DISNEY's chicken little

LITTLE TOWN HEROES

Adapted by Cary Okmin
Illustrated by Samantha Hollister
Designed by Disney Publishing's Global Design Group

A GOLDEN BOOK • NEW YORK

ISBN: 0-7364-2332-X

www.goldenbooks.com
www.randomhouse.com/kids/disney
Printed in the United States of America
10 9 8 7 6 5 4 3 2 1

A year ago, Chicken Little thought the sky was falling, so he warned the whole town.

It seems that it was really an acorn,
not the sky, that fell on his head!

Buck is Chicken Little's dad. He wishes everyone would forget his son's mix-up with the acorn.

Some people in town think Chicken Little is crazy.
They point at him and make him feel bad about himself.

Even though Chicken Little always seems to have bad luck, he still hopes things will soon change for the better.

Foxy Loxy is in Chicken Little's class. She is one mean fox.

As usual, luck is not on Chicken Little's side today.
He misses the school bus, and Foxy drops acorns in his path.
Help Chicken Little get to school.

FINISH

BUS

START

On his way to school, Chicken Little falls in some gum.
He is happy when he gets back up . . . until he notices
that his pants are missing.

A soda-pop rocket gives Chicken Little the boost he needs to get into school without being seen.

During the school day, Chicken Little's friend Abby convinces him to try talking to his dad about the bad moment with the acorn.

Later, in gym class, Foxy knocks Abby down
in a game of dodgeball.

Chicken Little stands up to Foxy.

Chicken Little and his friends will do anything to help each other.
Can you find all the friends' names in the puzzle?
Look down, forward, backward, and diagonally.
Each name is hidden twice.

ABBY RUNT FISH

```
R  G  F  I  S  H
T  N  U  R  T  R
D  E  Y  Q  H  U
O  L  N  B  S  N
A  B  B  Y  B  T
P  H  S  I  F  A
```

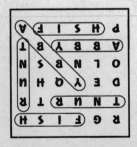

Fish, Runt, and Abby try to help.
Goosey scares them away.

But it's too late. Chicken Little is in trouble again!

Chicken Little's school principal has a talk with Buck.
He thinks Chicken Little causes too much trouble.

Chicken Little wants to be a baseball hero just like his dad.

Chicken Little tells his dad that he wants to make him proud
by playing a new sport.
To find out what it is, use the code to fill in the blanks.

E	B	L	S	A

_____ _____ _____ _____ _____ _____ _____ _____

ANSWER: Baseball.

Foxy is the star of the baseball team. She doesn't think
Chicken Little can play as well as she can.

The score of the big game is tied when
Chicken Little finally gets a turn at bat.
He hits the ball on his third try!

Chicken Little gets a home run and wins the game!
He's the team's new star!

Chicken Little celebrates his big day. He's the town hero!

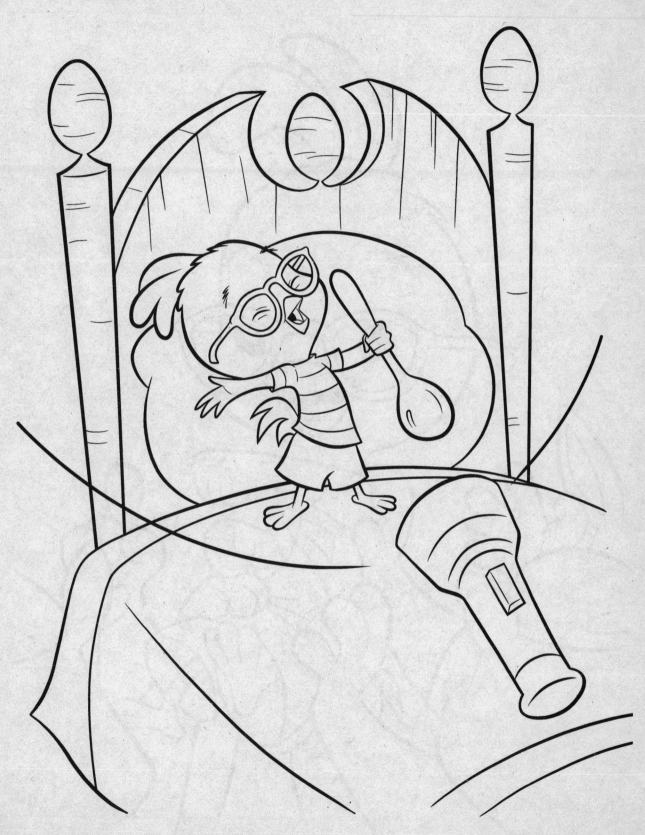

Now the people in town won't make fun
of Chicken Little anymore. Buck is proud of his son.

Chicken Little really wants to keep making his dad proud.
As he wishes upon a star to keep his luck going,
the star gets closer and closer to him.

When the star lands in his room,
Chicken Little thinks the sky is falling again.

Chicken Little's friends come over to help him figure out what the strange object is. Abby thinks it may be something that fell from a plane.

Fish presses a button on the strange thing, flies out the window,
and zooms across the sky!

Chicken Little, Abby, and Runt chase their friend.
They follow him to the town baseball field, and as they watch . . .

. . . a spaceship lands and aliens scamper into the woods!

Finally, the gang spots Fish—and he's in the top of the spaceship.

Chicken Little, Abby, and Runt go into the ship
to save their friend. Inside, it is strange and scary.

Runt sees Fish—but he looks like a skeleton on a slime screen!
Fish waves to his friends to let them know he is okay.
Now the friends are together again.

A small furry thing starts following Chicken Little and his friends.

It looks like the aliens who live on the ship
have plans to destroy many planets.

Starting with the letter E, circle every other letter
to find out the name of the next planet they will attack.
Then write the letters that are left on the lines below.

EYAGRLTXH

_ _ _ _ _

The friends want to warn everyone in town about the aliens' plan to destroy Earth. Chicken Little closes the door as the aliens chase them from the ship.

Help Chicken Little and his friends get to the bell tower
so they can ring the bell to warn their town about the aliens.

FINISH

START

ANSWER:

Chicken Little rings the bell!

The aliens don't like the loud sound it makes.

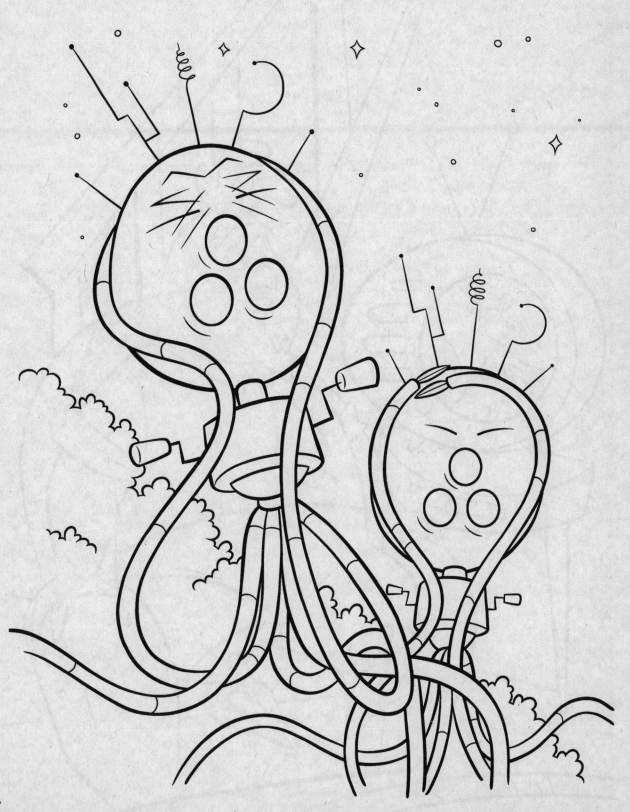

Buck is relaxing at home when he hears the bell ring.
He worries that Chicken Little may be causing trouble again.

Chicken Little warns the mayor about the aliens, then tells everyone in town to follow him to the baseball field.

By the time everyone gets to the field, the spaceship is gone.

Buck is upset that Chicken Little
has made everyone worry for no reason.

Chicken Little tries to tell his dad what happened,
but Buck doesn't believe his story.

A little alien has been left behind!

The next morning, Buck tells everybody in town
that he's sorry for the trouble his son has caused.

Chicken Little's friends try to cheer him up.

Suddenly, the alien child arrives. The only one who can understand him is Fish. He explains that the child misses his parents. Chicken Little wants to help.

Buck runs outside. He is scared when he sees spaceships filling the sky. Now *he* thinks the sky is falling!

Chicken Little tries to explain to Buck that the spaceships are looking for the missing alien. Buck doesn't believe him.

Meanwhile, the scared alien runs away!

Chicken Little tries to catch the alien. Buck is worried about his son's safety and chases him. He doesn't believe that the aliens won't hurt anyone.

Inside the town's movie theater, Abby tries to warn Buck and Chicken Little that more spaceships are coming. But they are arguing about the acorn mix-up that happened a year ago.

Chicken Little pulls back the curtain to show his dad
the baby alien. He convinces Buck that the alien is not going to
hurt anyone. His father finally believes him.

Now Buck and Chicken Little can work together
to get the lost alien back to his parents.

Chicken Little's friends want to help.
They race to the spaceship on top of City Hall.

The alien's parents are happy to see him,
and they zap him onto their ship.

At first, Chicken Little and his dad are scared
of the big furry aliens.

One of them speaks in a very big voice.

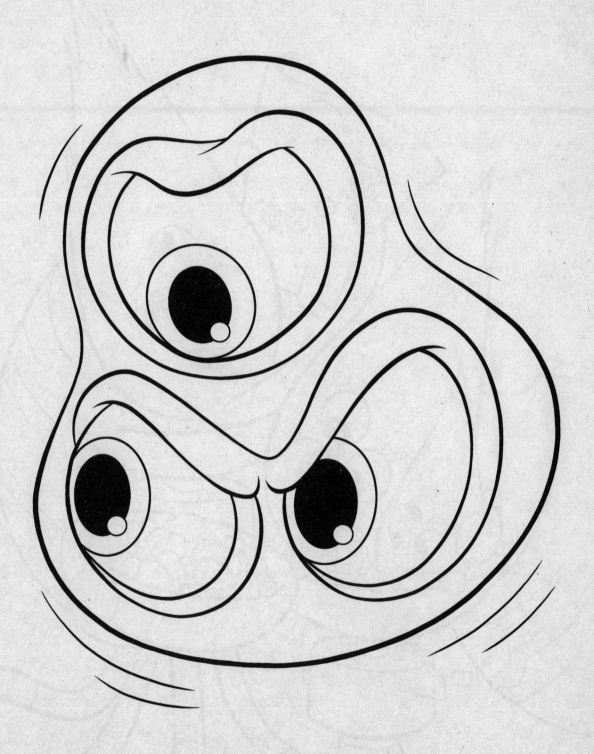

But then they find that the parents aren't really that scary.
The parents explain that they had stopped in Oakey Oaks
to pick acorns when their son wandered off the ship.

The people of Oakey Oaks are thankful that Chicken Little saved them from aliens. Now he is the star of his own movie!

Buck is very proud of his son.

And Abby is proud to call Chicken Little her best friend!

The whole town celebrates its new little hero!